Both in Abundance

Fantasy Short Stories

JH Tomen

ISBN: 979-8-9862909-2-8

For Isabelle

How will we become if we do not first learn to be?

et tui amóris in eis ignem accénde
renovábis fáciem terræ

Edits by Leona Skene
Cover by Karl Nilsson

The River

It took me a long time to remember being human. At first, I was simply a whirl of sensation, a prism through which an infinite light seemed to pour. But slowly, imperceptibly, I began to sense a pattern to the oneness in my mind. And as light gave way to shadow, contrast distilling into nuance and sound entering the silence, I began to notice the boundaries of my being.

I'm a river spirit, of course, though you already knew that. However, the first time we spoke, I failed to mention *which* river. I belong to — or *am*, I suppose — the Kuwan River, though it hasn't been called that in a long time. You might not have even realized it *had* a name, given how polluted it's become. But if you think it took me a long time to remember my origins, it took me even longer to remember those basic facts. Disinvestment, even pollution, are fragile human words, and at first, I only knew filth — or perhaps the rarity of its absence.

Strangely, it seems my soul has anchored in a particular stretch of the river, the segment near your flat where the water passes through concrete, beside the playground wedged between the factories. If I try hard enough, I can vaguely sense the larger river, the outlines of its banks as it winds throughout the kingdom. I could be simply reading the water's memory — the currents carrying fragments of some other soul further upstream — but whatever the feeling is, I know I fit within a greater whole.

I was sitting in that oneness, floating in its infinity, when I suddenly remembered what became of me. A…sickness, sudden and brutal as it removed me from the mortal coil. There hadn't been much time, but by the end, I think I had realized where things were heading, the worry on the doctor's face too clear. I had begged my family to scatter my ashes in the ocean, my brief holidays from the toil of the factory always spent by the sea. What happened next, I suppose, is easy enough to understand…

The factory offers no bereavement leave, and bus fare to the ocean is often hopelessly out of reach without scrimping and saving — something a sickness would make an even bigger impossibility than normal. My family must have scattered me in the river, in this stretch of concrete and filth, perhaps hoping my soul would find the ocean as it wound toward the shore. And maybe they were right… Perhaps I made myself this anchored spirit, unwilling to let go and end up something freer, a single fragment in a soup of other souls.

Still, I truly feel no bitterness. When the sun gets low in the sky and the factory lets out for the day, I sit and listen to the people as they pass. Sometimes, if the weather is nice, a young couple might walk by, laughing as they travel holding hands. I like to listen to their plans, their voices gushing as they trace their hopes and dreams. Even now, as my human self is pulled away, I find myself hoping for them too. Perhaps someday young couples will realize how fervently I wish them well — finding some correlation between good luck and wishing at my banks — and they'll start a shrine, draping offerings on my banks.

Still, that's a story for a different time. I may be here a thousand years, and my concept of time is quickly fading. What I know now, is that you have come, and I'm glad to see you. It feels like just yesterday when you first came to me, even if today and yesterday no longer hold much meaning. Still, to stick your hand into the filth just to see if I was real… I thank you for your courage.

At least, you don't seem afraid. You have no way to respond to my monologue, of course, though I sense no agitation in your soul. Unless you count…the *question*. I can sense it in the center of your mind, the thing that's driven you above all else. Ever since that day, even as you've grown, married, fought alongside the helpless in the factory, you ask: *Why me?*

I'm afraid I don't know. Which isn't to say there's no purpose to the thoughts I've shared. Why am I a river god? Why are you a human? Why do our souls crisscross this same stretch of concrete, whirling around each other amidst the savage chaos of time? Being part of a river, even as I lose my sense of time, I think somehow I can *feel* it more fully.

And the secret of time is this — it only exists when you will it to. In many ways, time is a circle, and we're bound up together in it like pieces of a bird's nest, like twigs and strings folded into a whole.

I'm sorry. I can sense your confusion. I promise I'm trying to put this in a way a human mind can understand. Here is what I mean to say: Whether you lived or died that day did not matter on the infinite scale. Whether or not my river is polluted, whether the apartment buildings stand, even whether the factory makes its iron fittings that will rust away in a hundred years' time — none of it matters. And yet...*everything* matters. Do you see what I mean? Why else would rivers have souls? Why else would lovers hold hands? Why else would humans stare out at the stars?

So when you fell into my waters, a foolish child playing outside the factory school, at first I was simply curious. Here was an agent of change, something to break my surface and stir up my muck. But quickly, as the lilies pulled at your ankles and the water filled your mouth, I saw you were in danger, and it...*pulled* at my soul. The soul I thought so passive, so removed from human life, could suddenly *feel* something.

Before then, I hadn't known I could contact humans — the way we're doing now. But with all my might, I reached for you. The moment I touched your soul, I saw confusion and fear, but also wonder. Even as a child, I could sense a depth to you that wouldn't go away. So I pushed. I pushed with every ounce of my meager power, and somehow it was enough. I created a wave to push you to the banks, until I could hear your ragged breaths again, the shouts of your teacher looking for you, and I knew you'd be alright.

This is the truth: there is some light far greater than our agony, and even in the darkness, *something* within us reaches out for it. Even amidst the filth and degradation, amidst the sadness and striving, there is light. In light, there can be no darkness, and so I have to believe the light may yet prevail. Will it correct the universe while you still breathe and while I still cling to these waters? That I can't answer. It could take eons or it could take a single day, but so long as we can feel that light, it means there's a purpose to each step we take. I don't know why I'm here, but I know I was grateful to ease your suffering, just as I know you're grateful to ease your people's.

You ought to go now. I can't in good conscience let you touch this water any longer. The surface alone contains seventeen carcinogens, only twelve of which humans are aware of. But I'll be here. Tell your children of me, if you desire. And one day, when you're victorious, I hope your grandchildren — or perhaps your grandchildren's grandchildren — will be able to swim here. Whether they worship me or not, I'll tell them of you, and I'll tell them of the light.

The Pond

I walked into the woods one day, on the verge of leaving everything behind. I looked back at the village in the early light, every chimney but mine weaving thin columns of smoke into the air. The inn was locked, the shutters on the tavern closed. My customers, few that I had, may have been disappointed, but if I didn't find the pond, it wouldn't much matter. I had packed enough to cross the mountains and simply wouldn't return. Eventually, the mayor would hold a vote, and the inn could be sold off.

I moved carefully through the forest, as eager to avoid leaving footprints as I was to preserve the tiny budding mushrooms that had appeared with the spring rains. As I walked under the early leaves of kirik trees, the only sound I could hear was the swishing of my pack and the breathing of the wind. Despite having gone so many years without use, my pack didn't feel heavy. It simply *was,* like another limb.

Would I find the pond? I thought of Kerin and the way the others had laughed at his story when he'd come back from the mountains. He'd left the village a few months later, but he hadn't seemed defeated or ashamed. In fact, he'd smiled wider than I'd ever seen. And when his cart passed by, all of his belongings strapped down for the road, he shook my hand.

"I hope you find it, too," he said, his eyes knowing. "You were always kind, and I think they'd take you in if you reached them."

With that, he'd ridden off for T'eru Plain, and no one had heard from him since, not even the tinker from over the river who mended our pots in the fall.

I climbed until midday when the sun was high, though it seemed to offer little heat up in the mountains. I climbed west, past the Old Man's Face, the weathered limestone covered in lichen. Kerin had said he'd followed the path of the sun. As I went back under the canopy, I started to feel foolish. Perhaps there was nothing out here, after all? Still, something kept me moving. I had nothing to lose, right? If I was leaving the village anyway, it mattered little if I went west or east.

Finally, though, somewhere north of Suri's Gap, I came upon a clearing, one I'd never seen before. Massive heron trees stood in a ring, spreading their sage green heads into the sky. In the center of the clearing was a hollow, its edges lined with stone, and in the middle was a single white lily, its petals already in bloom despite the spring chill.

I stood at the edge, watching. This was a *magic* place. And as I waited, torn between staying and going as the wind whispered overhead, I felt a fool again. What was I doing tempting the gods? Was my life really so bad I needed to go rooting around the woods? It reminded me of the story my pa used to tell, about the man who became a wolf, losing his life on the farm because he dreamt so hard of leaving it.

"You've come," a voice said.

I looked up, finding a woman standing before me. Or perhaps woman was the wrong word... She was made of light, a gentle blue that shimmered at the edges. She was incredibly beautiful too, though not the kind men in the tavern liked to boast of, laughing about stolen kisses on Middle-Night. This was the beauty of a boy looking up at his mother, knowing there was no one else in the world so lovely.

"We thought you might," said another voice, a woman who had appeared on the right side of the lily, her light a pinkish haze.

"We *hoped* you might," said a third, this one a soft green. They stood in a triangle around the flower, their eyes — or where their eyes would have been — seeming to linger on me.

"What are you?" I asked. "The stories, I..." I paused as the words — the honest words — came to me suddenly, my mouth seeming to say them without meaning to. "I think I'm afraid." Still, looking into that light, I didn't want to run, couldn't bear the thought of leaving.

"Fear not," the blue one in the center said. "We are the pond, and you are welcome here. Come."

She motioned for me to enter the clearing, and I did, my fear completely gone. There was a...rightness to the place, the magic too soothing to be of ill intent.

As I stepped closer, the women closed around me, guiding me forward until I was standing just before the lily. The blue one lifted a hand, touching my forehead. She lowered her head, as if thinking, as a warmth spread through my mind.

"You blame yourself," she said, looking back up.

"For your wife," said the green.

"When she was lost," said the pink.

"But nothing is ever really lost," the blue finished.

"I…"

I closed my eyes, feeling the truth bubble up in me again.

"Yes," was all I managed to say.

Images of her came back, ones I'd thought I'd forced away, of her sick in bed, coughs racking her very bones. My walk through the cold for the medicine, the medicine not working. And then…emptiness. The inn feeling cold, a cold no fire could banish. But with the blue woman's hand on my forehead, the cold no longer touched me.

"This is not your fault," she said, her hazy image smiling. "Light begets light. Day becomes night becomes day."

"You are one," said the green, "and so small you forget you are many."

"But no leaves fall from the branch as it sways," said the pink. "There are many worlds, both within and without, and they hold both love and time in abundance."

"Rain pools in the pond," the blue said, nodding. "And *we* do not forget what is forgotten."

I didn't understand what they meant, but as I opened my mouth to ask, the blue woman took me by the hand.

"Come," was all she said. The three of them swept me up, holding my arms and hands as they eased me onto the grass so my head was at the base of the lily. The blue one knelt beside the flower, putting both hands on my forehead. The green sat by my side with her hands over my heart, and the pink held my feet, removing my boots as my heels connected with the soft earth.

For a moment, there was only silence, the warmth of their hands pouring into me as a gentle breeze lapped at the trees overhead. My breath seemed to come on its own, in time with the blood from my heart, the wind itself filling me with air. The women let out a deep breath as one as they began to whisper, their voices quiet yet somehow filling my mind.

"You are loved," the blue said.

"You are worthy of love," said the green.

"Your love is enough," finished the pink.

They continued to repeat those words, unchanging, neither hurried nor slow, simply saying them again and again. The heat continued to fill me, so much so that at first I didn't notice the water. But soon, it was all around me, and I realized I was floating. I opened my eyes to find the clearing filled with water, a perfect blue pond rocking gently against the stone basin. But still, I felt no fear. In fact, I was sleepy, so sleepy I could barely keep my eyes open.

"You are loved," the blue said.

"You are worthy of love," echoed the green.

"Your love is enough," finished the pink.

Memories of my wife came to mind, but they were good ones, ones I'd forgotten as I pushed to forget the bad. Her face, smiling, our walks in the woods. The way she danced when the fiddler rode in from T'eru Hill, as if she were a bird in spring hopping from foot to foot. I remembered the first time I held her hand and kissed her lips, things so easily forgotten as the years of marriage piled high.

"You are loved," the blue said.

"You are worthy of love," echoed the green.

"Your love is enough," finished the pink.

Something bubbled up inside me, and laughter spilled out, uncontrollable. I shook with it, though the women held me steady, my smile growing wider, the muscles aching at the forgotten feeling. When the laughter finally faded, I felt lighter, even lighter than I did floating on the water. And still I laughed, chuckling to myself as I fell asleep.

———

When I woke, the water and the lily were gone, but I was still lying in the clearing, a ring of silver cups flowering around me in the grass. I looked up at the heron trees, the sky now a perfect blue, a mirror of the pond I had floated in. I looked at it, and I smiled.

The Well

I frowned, staring at the white flower in my hand. It had come off my cilantro, the perfect patch of clover-like green from a week earlier turned into…this. It reminded me how little I knew of this place — or the person I inhabited, for that matter. What was this vegetable really, and why had I planted it in the first place?

I reached for the little black box in my pocket, holding my thumb over the circle until it chimed, the lights coming alive as a picture of a dog appeared. The dog, at least, I understood. It had been at the man's house when I appeared, wagging its tail in the same way dogs had in my time. I had no idea what its name was, but it was a good sport, following me even now around the garden, its tail still wagging.

I held my thumb down, until the ghost's voice appeared, asking me what I needed help with.

"Why are there flowers on the *cilantro?*" I asked, my tongue still fumbling over the syllables. I had found the name the week before, written neatly on a card beside the plant. And I'd walked to a nearby grocer's — braving the speeding hell-chariots zipping down the street — to ask them what it was.

"Cilantro?" one of the clerks had asked, scratching his head. "It's just, like, an herb? Maybe try it sometime?"

So I had, returning to the garden and sampling it. I knew most of the other vegetables the man had planted in his garden, I just hadn't ever seen this one before, its seeds never making it to the island before I left.

"If not tended to properly," the ghost woman's voice read, "cilantro will bolt, growing white flowers that eventually turn into coriander."

Coriander! Now that I *had* tried, brought to the island on a ship. But that had been dried and ground — not to mention traveling hundreds of miles to reach me in the village. And to think it came from a plant like this, a common herb a stranger would grow for his enjoyment! At least he was growing things at all. People seemed to have paved everything in this time, man's obsessive conquest of nature in my time finally reaching its fulfillment.

Still, as I thought about whether or not I had tended to the cilantro properly, I felt an immense wave of sadness roll over me. I felt guilty in a way I never had before, as if I'd done something truly awful. But by the looks of things, the man had plenty of food still stored inside, the garden of little consequence compared to the bounty of this place. But this mind I found myself in seemed to have a will of its own, his thoughts rising up unbidden even as they weighed upon my soul.

I pinched the bridge of my nose, waiting for the thoughts to pass. How had I come to inhabit this man, of all people? The witch had warned me, of course.

"You cannot control magic this powerful," she had said, even as she counted my gold. "A visit to the days to come can only place you briefly in the soul of another, and when you return, your memories will be vague at best. I cannot tell you who or where. I can only trace the water and send you where it flows. Whether you are king or criminal, whether man still walks the earth, this I cannot say. Is this knowledge you seek really that valuable to you?"

Still, even as she asked me, she'd known I would say yes, had seen the hunger in my eyes. As a man of science, I wanted to know, of course. But for Lina, for everything I had lost when she died, I *needed* to know. Perhaps it was chance that brought me to this man, but I still hoped it was fate. After all, like the witch had said: "the spirit knows what it seeks even when the mind does not."

I opened my eyes, going back into the house. I took up the strange jar I had found earlier. It was orange and lighter than glass, and held what seemed to be some kind of tincture hidden within a gelatinous shell. They seemed important, standing in the center of this man's kitchen, presumably his name written on the bottle.

Sertraline, it read. *Take two daily.*

Even having trained in alchemy, I had never heard the name before. But whatever it was, I had been here for days already without taking it. I took one of the shells in my palm, holding it in the sunlight. Perhaps it would show me something, guide me toward whatever it was my soul had sought here, traveling on the witch's power.

I tilted it into my mouth, swallowing. Leaving the garden for the moment, I wandered back through the man's house. The place was longer than it was wide, the bright light of the kitchen giving way to a cavernous hallway leading to the front of the house. I came into a sort of great room, standing before a pair of wide bookshelves. I had seen them the first night, when I awoke in the house, but it had been dark then, and I hadn't figured out how to light the strange glowing lamps until the morning.

Directly in front of my eyes was a book with an orange cover, the binding somehow smoother than leather as it reflected the light. *Studies of Obsessive-Compulsive Disorder* was printed on the spine. I pulled it out, finding pinkish tags sticking out from the pages at random intervals. I opened it to one in the middle as I started to read:

— such that comorbidities are extremely common with OCD, afflicting some ninety percent of patients. These ailments range from anxiety and depression to personality disorders, often in the presence of complicating post-traumatic stress. This leads me to believe there may be some altered structure in the mind connecting all such disorders in ways genetic and behavioral that the current DSM does not describe with complete accuracy.

I felt so…adrift in this time, a man in a river who'd never learned to swim. Still, even as I barely knew half the words on the page, something stuck out to me: the *structure* of the mind. It seemed even in this man's pain — each twinge of guilt turned into a mountain along with who knew what other maladies — he had come to answer my prayers.

I thought of Lina. The beauty of her voice, the wonder in her eyes. Even on her darkest days, she had been filled with light, kinder than anyone I knew. It seemed the power of her mind, the depth of her creativity, had simply come at a cost. There was no demon lurking on her shoulder, no ghosts sinking into her flesh. What if those priests had never heard her whispering to herself in the gardens? What if I had been able to save her, to ease her troubles with some tincture like the kind this man had?

A tear fell onto the page, and I hastily wiped it away. I could feel my pain when I returned. For now, I had no way of knowing how much time the witch had bought me, how much I'd be able to research before I lost this form, this anchor to another time.

I was putting the book back on the shelf when a loose piece of paper fell out, fluttering to the floor. I picked it up, turning the weathered scrap over in my hand. A quick note had been scrawled in the man's hand. *Moral scrupulosity,* it began, the word underlined. *I hate myself, but I am alive. I am enough.*

And perhaps he was…

I walked back out to the garden, feeling more solid than before. It seemed I had come to the right place, even if I didn't know exactly what that meant yet. I walked toward the well beside the garden, lowering the bucket to water the plants. I looked down into the pool below, its surface rippling in the darkness as it reflected the sky. Was this the same ancient well from the past, the one outside the witch's hut? Or was this just another convenient source of water, linked to my home through a thousand random flows?

Perhaps it didn't matter. It was too much to count anyway, too much for a single mind to fathom. But I saw a way forward all the same. Whenever the water saw fit to take me home, even if I remembered little else, I would remember this. There was something sacred in us, something untouched even by this structure of the mind. And even with Lina gone, others would remain. I would find them, and I would see them as they were.

The Rain

What is a mind? Is it truly another? Or is it just a piece of *us*, fragments of a whole, kaleidoscoping to infinity?

How was it that men became so eager to die? Not all of them, of course. The cries of agony from the battlefield as the crows circled above was proof enough of that. But some men on the field had had the look, the same one they surely saw in his eyes. They had seemed ready, glad even, when the sword slipped in. There was a…certainty in the permanence of death, a rest that finally came to scoop you up, to take you away from the burden of your life.

But that was only one side of the story, of course. Life seems fleeting to men, but it's just as permanent as death, just as relentless — and in some ways, even more so. Because even in an empty grave, filled with nothing but bone and rock, there's *potential*, the possibility that life could just as easily spring up again. Even if one man's life is nothing more than a cresting wave, the ocean remains, along with the promise of more: more suffering, more joy, more…everything.

Lord Piroln dropped the dead man's gauntlet, standing as the rain continued to fall, forming a river on his face. He hadn't found the Sign of Erinelt yet, but it would be there. As he stared off into the mist, though, all he could see was the subtle weave of power, orbs of life and death whirling around each other. The death was obvious enough. It looked like flakes of ash, little pieces of loss released into the air. But unlike ash from a fire, which rolled about randomly on the wind, death had a specific rhythm, each piece flowing in the exact same way.

The life was more surprising. Like little dots of light, they seemed thickest where dead men were heaped the highest. The priestess seemed to think they were attracted to each other, life and death. But it could have also been the grass, the ground beneath the dead drinking in the blood and rain, eager to grow new flowers some day when this battle was nothing but bones. But life and death, as off-putting as they could be, were at least natural. What worried him was the shadow, pooling on the ground like an oily fog, coalescing in the places where a death had ended in hate. It didn't float away, didn't spin on the wind. It simply roiled like a stormy sea, looking for somewhere to go.

"We're running out of time, my lord," a scout said from behind him. "Just got a report of silver swords on the western flank."

"I know," Lord Piroln said, taking his sword from the ground. "We'd best be gone."

He could do nothing about the shadow now. He wasn't talented enough with the light to banish it, and the priestess still hadn't found the one she was looking for, the one who could wield the true sword. Still, there was work he *could* do. Someone had to be her eyes, and he would do it, even if it meant dying in the rain far from home.

———

Terisole trimmed a bush, her hands carefully edging down the long green stalk. She tried to do it in the way she had been taught, not taking off too many leaves while still promoting their growth. Its large white flowers, like bursting stars, were in full bloom, their fresh scent overpowering the smell of rain on the horizon. She couldn't see them, of course, but even without her eyes she could sense their contours. They brimmed with light, fit to bursting as they strained toward the fading sun, eager to lap up the energy of the world.

She took a deep breath, reaching out with her mind until it encompassed the entirety of the garden. She could sense the long pool in the middle, cut from the stone and filled with lotus and lily pads. Hundreds more flowers crowded the edges of the water, their roots digging into the stone in search of the water. She had only been alone at the temple for six months, but it was getting difficult to take care of them all on her own.

Still, she struggled on. The flowers were the only thing she could use to defend this place. Only light could fight the shadow, and light required life. Of course there was light in the stone, deep in the bedrock, but she hadn't found her wielder yet, and she could only do so much with her meager powers. So she carried on, trimming and fertilizing from sunup to sundown in the hopes it would be enough. There was no denying it now; the prophecy was close at hand. She couldn't point to it exactly, but she could sense the evil, growing beyond the boundaries of her mind, like a cancer on the world, eager to destroy.

If only Lord Piroln would return. It was a miracle he could see as well as he could, but they needed the wielder. Such a heartbreaking irony her work was. They needed one with enough shadow in their heart to fight, but without so much that they became a vessel to that same darkness. Although, perhaps that was the irony of *every* life. Each soul born alone, separated from the Creator: they all had to walk the journey from darkness into light.

The priests had always liked to talk about destiny, but she didn't believe in predetermination. Even the prophecy, which had proved itself true time and time again, was only a thing of *eventualities.* After all, it was evil that followed suffering, not the other way around. It was something in them, something in the way they were created that drove the currents of the stream. Separation caused this suffering, the fragments of life cut off from the greater universe, without control, without hope. But just as their individuality created pain, it created promise, too. That fragment of light still yearned for the whole, and as they struggled through their pain — if they didn't lose themselves — humans often became something more. Light that made more light, hope that kept them marching home.

Terisole reached for a rose, purposely pricking her thumb with a thorn. She dripped the blood onto the stone, placing her forehead over it as she prayed. The time was coming when she would have done all she could. And then, she'd have to trust the light, trust it could do what she could not.

"Please," she whispered at the end of her prayer. "Please."

The rain began to fall, continuing its endless cycle. It rose from the ground toward the sky, pooling into pockets of life before falling again. And in each raindrop, she could sense the world. Humans were so much like the rain, each life straining as a single drop. But as they fell, they would pool, becoming streams that became rivers. One raindrop didn't feel like much, but it would be enough. It had to be.

The Flood

The flood had wiped away the land, leaving nothing but a wide furrow in the earth. It had torn through the valley, revealing the strata of the hillside, reds and yellows whirling where there had once been trees. But beside the razed forest, there had been nothing there, so I was probably the only woman who would ever lay eyes on it. Still, how long before the realms of men stretched even here, and the natural rhythm of life became a tragedy? A flood of that size would have destroyed the capital, leaving nothing but the palace on its hill.

Having looked long enough, I sat on the ground and closed my eyes, lifting myself into the air. They hadn't sent me to look at mud, after all. Assuming they'd really intended for me to come back at all… Once I was flying steadily, I opened my eyes again, surveying the land below. I had lost the monster's tracks in the rain before the flood, so it was back to aimless wandering until I found its trail again.

How long had I been in the wilds now? At least three months, constantly chasing something I could *sense* without getting any closer. Still, how much more could I take? Couldn't they have chosen another? Perhaps they were worried no one else could bond the monster, but the same darkness allowing me to sense the creature threatened to swallow me, pooling in the corners of my mind. If I didn't find it soon, there might be nothing left of me to bond.

But even if I did bond it successfully, could I really kill it? They hadn't given me much choice, of course: there would be no home for me if I failed. Still, the courtesans who'd ordered me here knew nothing of spirit bonding, nothing of the cruelty it would require to kill another living thing that way, monster or not. Not to mention what it would do to me when the connection was ruptured… It made me think of the flood, surging through the valley as the soil boiled around it. Would the creature see me similarly, some force of nature come only to destroy?

I just had to hope killing the beast wouldn't take my ability to fly. It was the only thing that was truly mine. Even with the dozens of others at the Owl's Temple, I was the only one who sat as she flew. Most of them looked like they were swimming, while Master Joris looked like someone who was still asleep. But when I let my soul fly, I was truly free, free to soar through the sky in any way I wanted. I'd heard that in the south they were joining fliers together, combining their winds until they could form a sort of ship, carrying humans through the sky.

If only I could do work like that. Humble, simple work, peaceful enough to let me finally mend, to stop gasping for air each night as I fell asleep. I suppose even if I lost my flight — and the walk back to the capital with the monster's horn didn't kill me — I'd have enough money to do whatever I wanted. Maybe I could open an inn in the south, and the fliers could bring my guests, dropping them from the sky as I waved from below, the fragrant smoke from my kitchens rising up to greet them.

I stopped suddenly, feeling something shift within my mind. I hadn't been paying attention, crossing over the mountains into the Saerif Plain. Grass stretched for hundreds of miles, the dagger-shaped teeth of the next range far off on the horizon. I closed my eyes, feeling for the monster's darkness with my mind. It still felt far away, but what had changed? I had learned to track it in my sleep, the feeling never far from me, so I could tell it was different. It must have— *It was coming toward me.* Coming quickly and getting closer, the monster no longer running away.

I couldn't see it yet but decided to wait, hovering a hundred yards above the ground. It was far larger than me, and if it already knew where I was, there was no doubt it would reach me soon. The sun began to descend while I waited, but after an hour or two, I could feel it. There was a shift to the air, its *presence* felt even before I heard it. And then, it arrived, a dark shadow on the horizon that grew constantly larger.

It was impossibly huge, larger than the palace itself. Its spiny back rolled like the jagged mountains beyond, its skin the color of earth and covered in scales. It had been blue once, hadn't it? Though it must have been younger then. They said it had destroyed the port in Alkitair, but it must have been a newborn, unused to living on land. I squinted at it, struggling to decide if it flew or crawled. Its body seemed to float above the ground, but it still used its claws, tearing at the earth as it propelled itself forward. It was actually quite beautiful at a distance, like a moving mountain grown tired of staying forever in one place.

Couldn't they just have left it here? I could feel the darkness in its heart, but it wasn't vengeful. It simply *was.* Like the depths of the ocean or the power of the flood, it didn't destroy out of desire: it destroyed out of need. But it had been an adult for some ten years already, and all that time it had stayed out here in the wilds. Perhaps it was simply its reputation, the thought it could return keeping the empress awake at night. Like the dark spot on my own heart, some things were far worse in the stillness of your mind.

Finally, it reached me. Instead of stopping, it swooped past me, circling me in the air before it came to rest, its eyes mere feet from mine. They were massive, pools of darkness easily five times my size, my reflection disappearing in their depths. It blinked slowly as it exhaled, its spirit suddenly pushing against my mind, probing me with its essence. It felt…sad, exhaustion weighing against its hulking frame. I presented my soul to it as well, allowing the dark imprint on my spirit to touch against its own. And in that moment, I knew I could destroy it. All I had to do was will it to die, to introduce my own brokenness into its soul. As shadowed as it was, the beast was a simple creature, and if it felt the full weight of a human heart, it would simply cease to be.

But I saw another path, too… In all the months I had chased after it, the monster had grown to know me. I could sense the outline of myself in its mind, along with a question. Would I join it? It wanted to be free, yes. But more than anything, it wanted to stop running. It wanted to become a mountain again, something that simply was. It was *man* who was the flood.

I thought of the future I had imagined for myself: leaving the temple, building the inn. It felt…hollow now. Even if I left the wilds, I'd still be running away. And as broken as I was, I had felt better these months, hadn't I? It was only worrying about what came after that gave me pause. Slowly, I flew forward, until I could see each individual scale on the monster's face. I reached out and touched it, allowing our minds to merge. Beyond the darkness, there was something else, something I hadn't noticed. There was *life.*

The Falls

"A poet in the time of war?" she asked.

"Precisely," I said, though she didn't seem convinced.

I continued down the path, leading her toward the waterfall. It was famous in these parts, though I couldn't tell you why. It was beautiful, sure enough — almost impossibly so — but weren't all waterfalls? Perhaps it was this walk that made it famous. It required a steep ascent through a channel in the stone, rising higher and higher until it emerged onto a cliff, facing the waterfall and the perfectly blue pool it emptied into.

"But there must be more to it than that, surely," she said from behind me, her voice short of breath as she worked to keep up.

It was actually rather impressive how well she climbed the path. She wore the robes of a court minister, sage green and cursedly woolen, not to mention the fact that they dragged well below her feet. She held them up by her hips, moving one sandaled foot after the other. She was really very pretty, with bright eyes and the curved nose of all capital women. She also had that…dewiness about her, the vitality of all the women — and men, of course — born after all the awfulness of the war. But alas, I could have been her father, not to mention her being above me in every sense — rank, upbringing, ability — so it was better not to think about her nose, let alone the elegant shape of her neck…

"I know," I said. "Everyone who interviews me says the same thing. They love to go on about the elegance of my words, the rhythm of my ballads — all of that junk. But you asked me *why* I became the poet I am today. And truly, it's simply a matter of timing."

"The time of war," she said.

"Yes," I said. I hope she was impressed that I wasn't out of breath in the slightest — a man my age! Maybe it would help her ignore the wrinkles around my eyes, though she'd probably just chalk up my *vigor* to the lifestyle of any uplander. "My first poem — accepted by the emperor, anyway — was—"

"The Ivy in the Grotto," she said, interrupting.

I stopped, quirking an eyebrow at her.

"Sorry," she said, her chest heaving as she stopped.

"No, no," I said, chuckling. "I just… Well, the other interviewers certainly didn't know that."

I walked on, frowning. She said she'd studied classics at the royal university, but I hadn't ever thought of myself as worthy of such scrutiny.

"Anyway," I continued, "the Grotto is decidedly not a seminal work of poetry. The meter is all wrong; my word choice is abysmal. But still, the emperor himself wrote my acceptance letter, and do you know what it said?"

This, she couldn't possibly know. Nowadays, every word uttered by the emperor was placed in the royal archives, but after the war, there wasn't *paper,* let alone a place to store it. In fact, he'd scrawled his response on a giant shell from the Dark Sea, his seal smudged lopsidedly on the twisted end. I turned to face her, but she shook her head, her eyes curious.

"He said, 'The people have lost enough, and I think you'll give them hope.'"

"The emperor said that?" she asked. Of course, she'd probably hadn't ever seen his face, even as high up in the court as she was. Now, she'd know him more as a god than a warlord, much less as someone who wrote his own letters.

"He did," I answered. "Things were…different then. But you see, that's my point. He and I agreed. The people needed hope. Things were harder then, darker. They — *we* — had been through enough."

I kept walking, letting her chew on that. Besides, the waterfall was close. Already, I could hear it. What had been a distant buzz before was growing to a roar, like the dragons of the Bal'helien. The mere thought sent a shiver down my spine, but I ignored it. The dragons were dead, carried to the grave by my men. Still, she deserved time to process. Even the young ones knew their share of grief. Even with childhoods unmarred by war, they grew up with parents gone, uncles and aunts missing eyes or legs. No one was untouched, and even her children someday — whichever lucky bastard got to make them with her — would know something of loss, even thirdhand, the deprivation of those years etched into our kingdom like the bones beneath my skin.

I thought of Xiera suddenly, sucking in a sharp breath as her face came back to me. I hadn't thought about her in months — save for my usual lamenting over wine in the gardens. I suppose the girl reminded me of her. Or rather, maybe I simply *wanted* her to remind me. Like my favorite motif, the moonlit woman, already in hundreds of my poems. But who was she really? A bit of artifice, of course, a way to let the reader find themselves within the verse, to play a bit with whoever they had lost. But who was she to me?

Sometimes I wished she really would come down from the moon to dance with me. But like my old teacher had once said: "*You* are the line you're looking for. The character you're spilling onto the page is just a part of yourself, the part you still crave after all this time, neglected and waiting."

And there was some truth to that. Xiera *had* been willing to dance with me, had held me closer than I'd ever been held, and still I'd let her go. There was a word for it in this beautiful region I'd settled in: *störishterin,* an ebehlin word, I think. It essentially means 'allergic to happiness,' and I suppose I am. But when Xiera looked me in the eye, offering me every happiness the world had to offer, I couldn't take it. I'd had enough killing, enough guilt. How could I say yes while knowing I'd only let her down? Far better to live in a false palace, surrounded by beautiful trinkets of my own design.

"—and so I guess my question is, why did you write that second poem?"

I shook my head, trying to leave the dreams behind me. Poor woman. How long had she been talking while I daydreamed? At least my back was to her, if only to conceal how unworthy I was of her company, how foolish a trip she'd taken for this interview. At least I'd caught the summary…

"Well," I said, "the second poem was about growth. I'd just gotten here — to the region, that is — and I suppose it was the first time I'd realized I would stay. As a magistrate, true, but as a poet, too."

Just then, we finally reached the top of the path, and the waterfall roared before us. She stepped up beside me, staring into the spray.

"Wow," she said, her voice barely audible above the raging water.

"I know," I said. "True beauty."

"*True* beauty?" she asked, finally breaking her eyes away. "I thought you would have had more of a grasp on beauty than anyone."

"No," I said, smiling sadly. "I'm just a mirror, and everything in my poems is passed through me. This…is the source. Something that has nothing to do with me. It's freeing really, to look at something and simply know that it's good, without having to obsess over what it means to you."

"Hmm," she said, stepping to the edge of the cliff to look down into the pool. For the first ten feet, it was completely clear, the rock visible as it disappeared into the darkness. Perhaps I wouldn't have understood it myself if she hadn't asked me. But now, I could *feel* the truth. I didn't write because I wanted to hold onto that beauty — letting go of Xiera was proof of what a sieve my heart had become. I wrote to show it back to them, the ones who still lived on, to show them a way out, a way forward, like the relentless rushing of the river.

"I'm sorry," I said, "you've found an old man lost in thought today. Have I answered enough of your questions? This won't make much of an archive, but I'll gladly give you any materials I have back at the villa."

"Oh, this isn't for an archive," she said, turning back to me. "I just wanted to get a feel for you. There's trouble in the east, and I've come to see if you're up to the task."

"And what task is that?" I asked.

She smiled, pulling a scroll from her bag and handing it to me.

"To hope," she said, "and make them hope with you."

The Sea

Why don't I ever think about you? Staring at the water, I finally did. But how many months had it been since the last time? It's only gotten rarer as the days go by. Not that I don't miss you. More than anything, I wish you were here. In a real, tangible way. I've grown up enough to know what people are and aren't. I know how sick you were, but I know how good you were, too. I don't miss an idealized version of you. I'm old enough to know how difficult it would have been if you'd stayed. But I know how truly good you were, too. And with all that human duality, all that darkness, I wish you were here anyway.

I leaned forward, putting another log on the fire. It wasn't dark yet, the sun only three-quarters of its way through the sky. But the fire felt nice against the salt breeze from the ocean. It was gray like the sky and endless, pushing toward the east where it merged with the curving of the world. Whichever world it was… I was losing track of how many days since I'd crossed over, but it was a nice place, as far as worlds go. I picked up my *serife,* the gold dial spinning endlessly against its crystal back. Empty. Completely and utterly empty.

Tarithe hadn't sent me here to sit on the beach, of course. She'd sent me to look for another keris stone. But you couldn't have keris without people, and so it seemed there was nothing for me to do until the portal opened — though whether it would be sending me to another shard world or bringing me home wasn't for me to decide. Still, you should always take a break when you can get one. Besides, after a hundred worlds — and even more reasons to use my sword — I could stand a bit of quiet.

Maybe that's why. Maybe I only think about you in the quiet. And why shouldn't I? Like the Ancient Mother, it's in the nothingness where you're closest to me. Like the ocean, boundary-less and infinite. That's what I like to think, anyway. *She took her life,* they said to me after it was finished. But it doesn't feel like you took anything. Somehow, it still feels like you gave. You made me who I am, built me brick by brick. You held me close, you read to me, you *delighted* in who I was. In a way I've never felt since and might never feel again. But even when I crave your closeness, I'll accept your distance, a far sweeter gift than any other I've received. I only hope I can make someone else feel that way someday.

I pulled the whiskey from my pocket, pouring a bit over the sand. Tarithe cared little for my rations — and even less for something like whiskey — but it felt right to spill some in your honor. I poured the rest into my mouth, tilting my face toward the sky as I closed my eyes, savoring the burn as it slid down my throat. I still hoped the next portal would be for home, but it felt right to be here, to find this place to think.

Tarithe seemed to think it didn't cost me anything to make my food. "Just do the little dance," she liked to say, as if conjuring the essence was a simple matter. But just like keris stone, the further you were from the Ancient Mother, the harder it was to conjure much of anything. I probably wouldn't be able to find anything on this barren beach, for example, and even in a more hospitable world, 'the dance,' as she called it, could still take more than an hour from start to finish.

I rubbed my face, standing from the sand. I didn't feel particularly hungry, which was a bad sign, but I may as well try. For whatever reason, hunger disappeared in the further worlds, as if the Mother's presence — or lack thereof — gave and took needs just as easily as their fulfillment. Sometimes I wondered what it would do to my life force, wandering about the fringes like this, but some questions were better left unanswered. Besides, if Tarithe didn't care about my whiskey, she probably wouldn't care if someday I simply didn't cross back through.

At least sand was an easy vessel. There was something about its granularity, so close to the rock it had come from, yet so far from the *aliveness* of soil that was easy to conduct. You taught me that, actually. Taught me everything I know. I remember now, for whatever reason, the first time you brought me to a beach to dance the sand. I'd been, what...ten? It was some time after the first time you'd left, I remember that much.

But when you returned, it was like you'd never gone. That's the way your presence was. More like the sun than the sea, actually — burning so bright there was no room for anything else. I didn't even ask what you'd been doing all that time you were away. Even as my questions had kept me tossing and turning all night in your absence, it simply hadn't mattered anymore once you returned.

I traced the lines of summoning, stooping over as I dragged my hands through the sand. It was tempting to use my foot — I knew enough about the shadows now to know the Ancient Mother didn't care much one way or the other about my sacrilege — but for whatever reason, I wanted to do things right. Maybe I just wanted to remember you a little better. They say memory *really* lives in the body, and hunched over like that, my fingers deep in the cool sand, it felt like I was back there with you. What was that beach called, again? *Cherishal?* It looked like this, actually.

Thankfully, the wind was relatively tame, and when I finished, the lines were still where I'd put them. The outline looked like a broken egg, a crack right down the middle that splintered into lightning shapes at the bottom. You had taught me this shape that day, didn't you? That was before Tarithe, before the guild or any of the others. This must have been the first shape I learned — really learned, anyway, drawing the shape over and over until I knew it by heart.

"Use this whenever you need me," you'd said, wiping the sand from my hair as I stood. "If you think of me, it'll call me, same as the Ancient One."

And maybe that was true. They do say that all mothers carry a bit of the Ancient's heart, after all. But then, when I'd drawn the shape in blood, desperate to get you back after you were gone, where had you been then? The elders punished me badly for that, by the way. But still, after hours of dancing in the rain, screaming out your name, you never came. *Beyond reach*, they'd said. *With the Mother, from which none return.*

Still, as I began the dance, moving my body along the lines, I found myself whispering your name. Even though it was food I needed, I still hoped you'd appear instead. Though how you would look was another question I could hardly dare consider. Would you appear older, as if you'd lived through all those intervening days? But what if you didn't age? I was still barely to your shoulders when you went, and in my mind, you're still bigger than me, still wrapping me up in your arms.

I danced harder than I ever have — before or since. I danced until sweat formed on my brow, cool in the sea breeze. And then, just as I was about to collapse on the sand, I felt a shift, the wind blowing toward the water instead of from it. I turned, my jaw dropping as a light appeared. Right at the point where the water met the sand, it started as a pinprick before it grew, spinning out until it became a swirling circle.

But then, it formed a door. Growing until it was about my height. So it wasn't you, after all… I brushed off my hands, walking toward the door as it opened. Maybe Tarithe would be on the other side, welcoming me home. But more likely than not, it was just another world, with another one beyond that. Still, before I walked into the light, I knelt down, scooping a bit of sand into my pouch.

"Maybe next time," I said, smiling sadly. Somewhere, there would be another sea, another horizon. And I'll think of you then. And when I call, I really hope you'll answer.

THE END